The Moonlit Princess
A Persian Cinderella Story

Retold by
Sarak Ardestani

Illustrated by
Whitney Mattila

ISBN: 1530561884
ISBN-13: 978-1530561889

For my readers,

May this classic piece of Persian (Iranian) culture find its way into your heart.

FOREWORD

The Moonlit Princess is based on the classic Persian fairy tale *Mah Pishooni* (ماه پیشونی). The literal translation of *Mah Pishooni* is "Moon Forehead." As you will read in the story, through a series of events, the main character will end up reflecting an image of the moon on her forehead.

The significance of the moon can be linked to an expression in the Farsi language, "Mesle Mah Memooni" ("You resemble the moon") or "Mesle Mah Memooneh" ("She's like the moon"). It is one of the greatest compliments you can give a woman or girl. This is because the moon historically symbolizes tremendous beauty and charm in Persian literature and culture.

Traditional Persian fairy tales such as *Mah Pishooni* were originally passed down orally in Farsi through the generations. As with many tales of its time, dating back hundreds of years, its exact origins are not well-documented. There are countless versions of this story that typically vary based on the region in Iran where the story was told and the political influences of the times.

This book retells in English an older version of the story and keeps true to it in most major aspects. In some modern versions of this story, the old lady is replaced by an ugly monster (dîv). The monster is self-serving and frightful compared to the old lady, who can be characterized as a fairy godmother figure in this version.

Once upon a time, in a land far away, lived a man named Khar-Kan, who collected wood in his village neighborhood. In the entire universe, the only thing of value in his life was his one daughter. His wife had already left this world, and he lived in a tiny house with his daughter, Mah.

Mah's teacher at school was especially nice to her because she knew that the girl did not have a mother. The teacher's husband had also left this world. Like Khar-Kan, she had one daughter who was the same age as Mah. The teacher took good care of Mah and easily found a way to her heart. The girl listened to everything the teacher asked. One day, the teacher asked the girl to set up a marriage between herself and Mah's father. Mah obeyed, and the teacher quickly married her father and became her stepmother. Mah was happy about this. She hoped the teacher would fill her mother's empty place.

But from the very moment the stepmother put her foot in Mah's house, she switched from acting one way to another, and became very mean to the poor girl. Meanwhile, Mah's father was nowhere to be found. Every day, before sunrise, he left early to collect wood to sell in the city, and by sunset he returned home tired.

The stepmother said horrible things about Mah, and her father did not know what to do. On many nights, the stepmother punished the helpless girl. Mah would not say anything about her troubles to her father because having her teacher as her stepmother had once been her wish.

One night, the stepmother said to Khar-Kan, "Why do you want to burden yourself by giving Mah free room and board? Let her go to work in the village and herd sheep." The father let the stepmother have her way and sent the girl away the next day.

Mah took the sheep and went to the fields. The following day, the stepmother gave her several large lumps of cotton and said, "So that you don't get bored while you're out there, spin this cotton into thread."

The girl did not say anything. She took the cotton and the sheep and went to the fields.

In the field, Mah sat under a tree and started spinning the cotton into thread.

Suddenly, a heavy wind came and swept up all of the cotton! Afraid of getting into

trouble with her stepmother, she raced after the cotton. A gust of wind tossed the

cotton into a well. Mah, puffing and panting, reached the top of the well. She looked

down as she tried to catch her breath. The well was dark and scary. The girl frowned

and asked herself, "What will I do now? If I return home without the cotton, my

stepmother will kill me!"

Trembling with fear, she climbed into the well. When she reached the bottom, she saw a narrow path. She walked and walked until she reached a house. Mah knocked on the front door, and an old lady opened it. The girl greeted her politely and asked, "Have you seen my cotton?"

The old lady replied, "Yes, your cotton is in my house. Come in and take it."

Mah entered the old lady's house. The house was very dirty and dusty. While the old lady went to bring the cotton, Mah grabbed a broom and started cleaning the house. She swept the floors and wiped away the dirt and dust. The old lady was very pleased with her help. She gave the girl the cotton and said, "My angel, may you always be lucky! You are such a kind girl."

"On your way back, there is a fountain. If black water comes out of it, do not touch it. If yellow water comes out of it, also do not touch it. But if you see the water is white and clear, wash your hands and face with it." The girl thanked the old lady for the advice and went on her way home.

Just like the old lady said, along the way Mah reached a fountain. The water pouring out of the fountain was black, so she waited and waited until the water became white and clear. Mah used the white water to wash her hands and face. Suddenly everything became light and bright around her, and she looked to her left and right with wonder. Mah peeked at her reflection in the water. An image of the moon twinkled on her forehead!

Fearful of how her stepmother would react, she tied a cloth across her forehead to hide the moon. At sunset, Mah returned home. Her stepmother asked, "Why have you covered your forehead?"

The girl put her hand over the scarf and said, "I fell on my way and hurt my forehead."

After the family had eaten dinner and Mah had gone to sleep, the sneaky stepmother wanted to see if the girl told the truth, so she gently removed the cloth from her forehead. The entire house lit up like daylight! The stepmother immediately woke the girl and said, "Oh naughty girl, you lied to me! Why do you have the moon glowing on your forehead?" She grabbed a stick and held it over the girl.

The girl began to cry and said, "Please don't hit me! I'll tell the truth."

The stepmother put down the stick and said, "Hurry up, Wicked One, explain yourself!"

Mah told her the whole story. Seeing the beauty of the moon, the stepmother said to herself, "I have to send my own daughter to the well to make a moon appear on her forehead, too."

The next morning she told Mah, "You don't need to go to the village today. My beautiful daughter will go in your place."

For the journey, the mother wrapped a whole chicken for the girl and said, "My daughter, go to the fields, take the sheep, and thread this cotton." She handed her the cotton. Mah's stepsister cried, "No, Mother, I don't like working!"

But her mother forced her to go. Mah's stepsister took the cotton along with the sheep and left for the fields. Out of laziness, she fell asleep under a tree. When she awoke and started eating the chicken, a huge wind came and blew the cotton into the well!

She dragged her feet as she followed after the cotton, and then slowly lowered herself down the well. She walked and walked until she reached the old lady's house.

Mah's stepsister banged loudly on the front door. When the old lady opened it, the girl jumped back and screamed, "Vah-vah, what a scary old lady!"

The old lady frowned. "What do you want?"

The girl said, "It's none of your business, you nosy old lady. Just tell me where the fountain is. I want to become pretty like my stepsister and have the moon twinkle on my forehead."

The old lady replied, "Take this path until you reach the fountain. When you arrive, if you see the water is white, do not touch it. If the water is yellow, also do not touch it. When you see the water is black, wash your hands and face with it."

Mah's stepsister walked until she reached the fountain and followed the old lady's advice. As black water poured out of the fountain, she washed her hands and face with it. When she finished splashing her face and looked at her reflection in the water, she saw a horn sticking out of her forehead!

Crying, she returned home and explained everything to her mother. The mother was angry and tried to cut the horn off with a knife. But no matter how many times she cut it, the horn kept growing back!

News about the girl with the moon on her forehead travelled and reached the ears of the prince. The prince sent several of his men to Mah's house. When the stepmother saw the men at her door, she ran to the kitchen and hid her stepdaughter in the oven. She returned to the door with her own daughter wrapped in a headscarf and said, "Here is the Moonlit Girl, take her to the prince."

When Mah's stepsister arrived at the castle, the prince removed her headscarf and saw her horn! Surprised and angry, he ordered Khar-Kan and his wife to be brought to his castle.

The prince demanded, "What kind of game is this? Where is the *real* Moonlit Girl?" The father was forced to explain the whole story. After learning the truth, the prince immediately rescued Mah from the oven, and then punished both the stepmother and the stepsister.

After Mah was freed, she fell in love with the prince and they got married. Once she became a princess, Mah shared her story with the kingdom to show how important it is to help those in need – and the magic it can bring. Everyone across the land listened to her, and they all lived happily ever after.

THE END

ABOUT THE AUTHOR

Sarak Ardestani, the daughter of Iranian-American parents, was born and raised in Virginia. She heard her first Persian fairy tale as a bedtime story at the age of six. Sitting at the foot of the bed, her Uncle Ali narrated the tale to her and her cousins. More tales later followed, and Sarak was drawn into the splendor of Persian stories.

Sarak earned her B.A. in English at the University of Mary Washington. She lives and works in Washington, DC. Her goal is to give new life to traditional Persian fairy tales and share them with the English-speaking world. Sarak's first children's book was "The Roly-Poly Pumpkin: The Untold Cinderella Story," and "The Moonlit Princess" is her second.

Made in the USA
Lexington, KY
05 May 2016